Well-known stories
to read and share

Written by Nick and Claire Page
Illustrated by Sara Baker and Katie Saunders

Contents

This is the story of a man called Joe,
and what happened in his shoe shop, long ago.
Ready to start? Away we go!
There's something else –
can you guess what?
Throughout this story,
there's a slipper to spot.

The Elves and the Shoemaker

Nick and Claire Page
Illustrations by Sara Baker

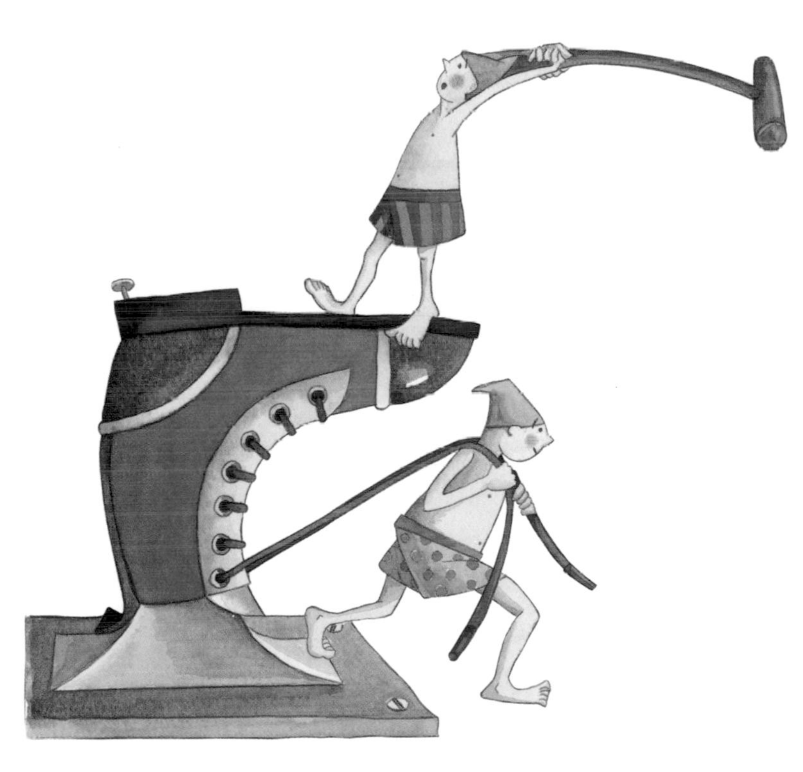

Once upon a shoe shop,
a long time ago,
lived a down-at-heel craftsman
called Cobbler Joe.

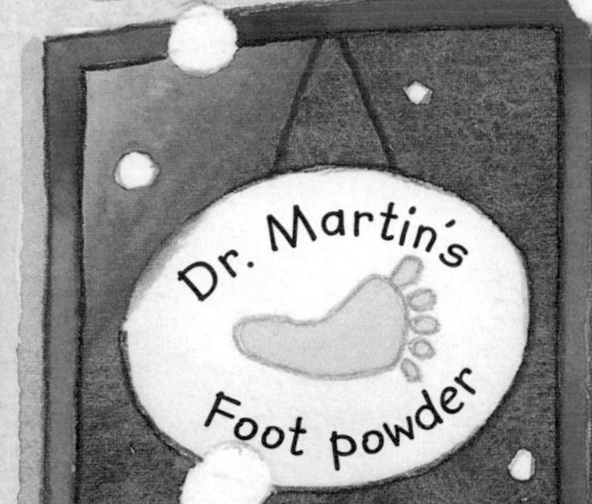

Heel and toe,
stitch and sew,
making boots
and shoes to go!

Very tired and hungry
was poor, old Cobbler Joe.
"There is nothing left to eat!"
declared his wife, Flo.

Joe was sad.
Things were bad.
Just some leather was all they had.

He cut a piece of leather,
enough for one small pair
and laid it on his workbench, left it there.
Shook his head, went to bed.
"Start on them tomorrow," old Joe said.

Early the next morning,
Flo told Joe the news,
"There's something in the shoe shop:
brand-new shoes!"

Heel and toe,
stitch and sew,
someone's done the work for Joe!

Joe put them in the window –
can you guess what?
A lady came and bought them;
paid a lot!
Said, "I'll go tell high and low:
buy your shoes from Flo and Joe!"

Joe and Flo had money –
and no time to lose,
bought some more fine leather
to make more shoes.
"Cut it right, leave in sight,
will it happen again tonight?"

Joe and Flo next morning, what did they behold?
TWO new pairs of boots there, waiting to be sold!

They were beauties. They were cuties.
Joe and Flo sold both those booties!

Every night, this happened, just the same.
When Joe left out the leather, new shoes came.

Sew and stitch, not a hitch,
Flo and Joe got very rich!

On Christmas Eve, at teatime, Flo says to Joe,
"Let's wait up and find out who helps us sew."
So they hide, eyes open wide.
What surprises there they spied!

As the clock chimes midnight,
singing to themselves,
there appear with toolbags,
two small elves.
Tip tap here,
tip tap there,
working in their
underwear!

Two elves with no clothes on,
working in the shop!
Sunrise comes,
they down their tools,
and off they hop.
Heel and toe,
stitch and sew.
"We must make them
clothes!" says Flo.

Joe and Flo made outfits;
left them on the table,
in boxes tied with ribbon
and a label:
"Now we know!
Thank you so.
To our friends,
love, Joe and Flo!"

When the clock struck midnight,
Joe and Flo looked on.
The elves unwrapped their outfits,
put them on!
"What a day!
It's our pay!
Now we can
be on our way!"

And that's where all this ended. The elves went away.
But Joe and Flo were rich now, so that was all OK.

OUR MOST POPULAR STYLE

Heel and toe, Flo and Joe,
once upon a *shoe shop*,
a long time ago.

This is a story of Coralie,
a mermaid princess living under the sea.
There's something else in this story as well –
on every page, can you spot the seashell?

The Little Mermaid

Nick and Claire Page
Illustrations by Katie Saunders

In a beautiful palace
under the sea,
lived a mermaid princess
who was called Coralie.
As she played with the gulls,
one gray, windy dawn,
she saw a small boat
that was caught in a storm.

Prince Roderick was fishing
for pearls in the sea,
when a wave hit the boat!
He fell in, "Quick! Help me!"
She rescued the prince,
brought him safe to the bay,
sang softly to wake him,
and then swam away.

Back at the palace, her head's in a whirl,
"I wish – how I wish – that I was a girl!"
Her sisters, called Laura and Flora and Dora,
said, "Why don't you go to see Seaweedy Nora?"

Now Nora was smelly and not very nice.
She liked to eat jellyfish, sea slugs, and lice.

At the back of her cave,
deep down in the ocean,
Seaweedy Nora
mixed up a dark potion.

Nora said, "Here, I can give you your wish.
Drink this, and you'll be a lot less like a fish.
Now pay me by filling this shell with your voice!"
So Coralie paid – there was simply no choice.

Jelly Fish

She drank up the drink (it smelled of fish eggs)
and when she reached land, her tail became legs!

Later, Prince Roderick sailed past her once more
and said to her, "Haven't I seen you before?"

But she couldn't speak,
so looked into his eyes.
She stepped into the boat,
and to her surprise,
the prince leaned toward her
to give her a kiss.
But Seaweedy Nora said,
"I must stop this!"

With Coralie's voice, she sang,
"Prince, come to me!"
and the prince, now enchanted,
jumped into the sea!

Coralie watched but could not say a word.
Then, on a rock near her, she spotted a bird.

The bird went and fetched
all of Coralie's friends –
seagulls and crabs,
and a lobster called Ben.
They pecked at old Nora
and broke the seashell.
Coralie's voice was released –
they had broken the spell!

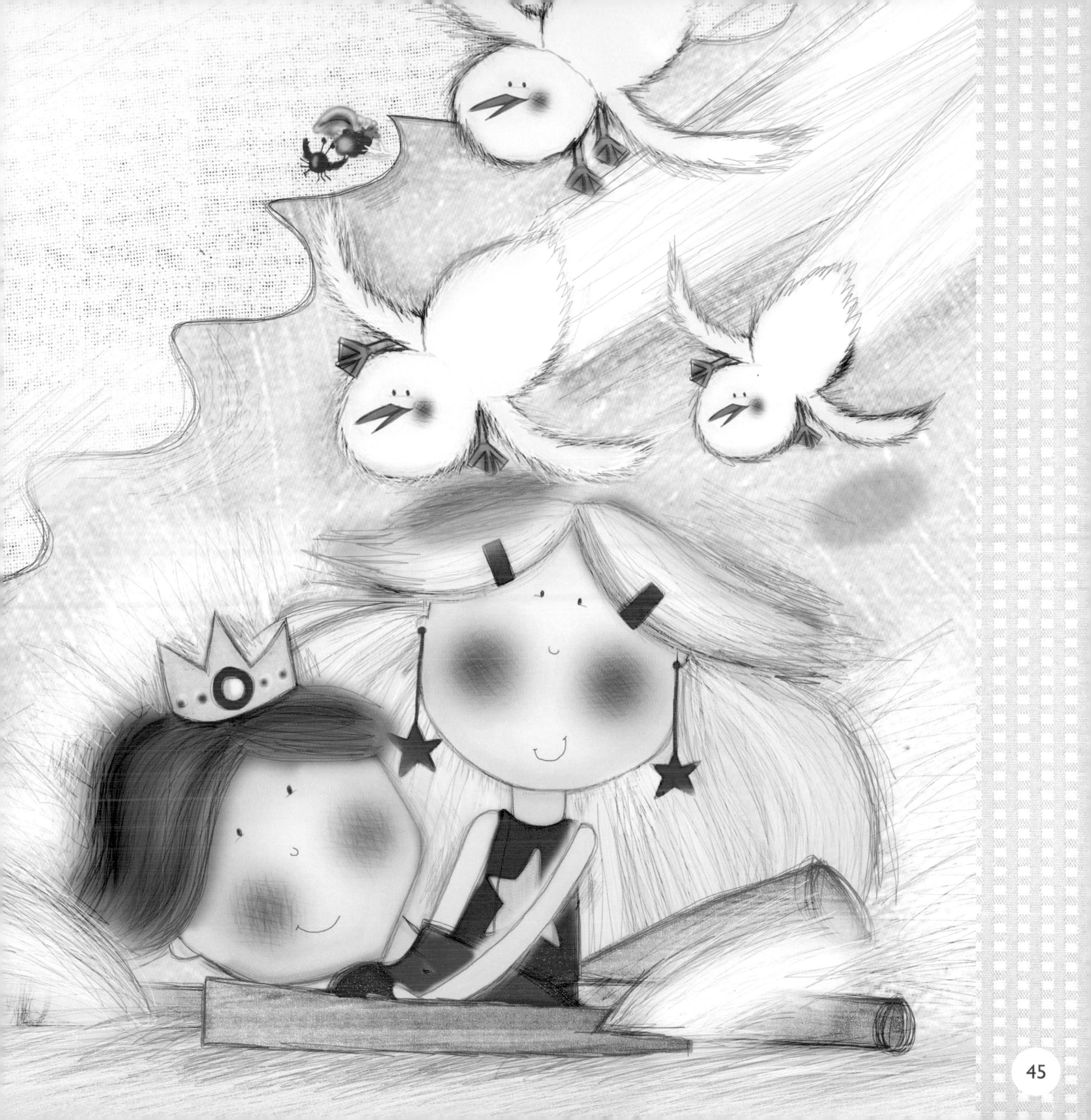

Seaweedy Nora was chased far away,
and the prince and the mermaid
were married that day.
Now the mermaid's a girl,
Coralie has her wish –
but sometimes she wishes
that she was a fish!

This is the story of Gingerbread Fred.
You can read it in a chair or read it in bed.
You can get someone else to read it instead!
There's something else – can you guess what?
On every page, there's a mouse to spot!

The Gingerbread Man

Nick and Claire Page
Illustrations by Katie Saunders

There once was a little old baker
and a little old baker's wife.
One day they baked a gingerbread man,
who magically came to life!

The name that they gave him was Gingerbread Fred.
And they said, "Don't go out on the street!
You are not a real boy, you're a cookie –
and that makes you yummy to eat!"

But before you could say
"JELLY DONUTS,"
their gingerbread son
had started to run!

And Gingerbread Fred said . . .

"Run, run, run, as fast as you can.
You can't catch me, I'm the gingerbread man!"

First, Gingerbread Fred reached a garden,
where a cat lay asleep in the flowers.
"MEE-WOW!" said the cat.
"Here comes breakfast! I've been
waiting for hours and hours!"

But Fred didn't wait –
he started to skate!

And Gingerbread Fred said . . .

"Skate, skate, skate,
as fast as you can.
You can't catch me,
I'm the gingerbread man!"

Next, Gingerbread Fred reached a farmyard,
where a dog was lying about.
"BOW-WOW!" said the dog.
"It must be lunchtime!
It's a gingerbread-man takeout!"

But before you could say,
"LEMON CHEESECAKE,"
Fred turned aside
and started to ride!

And Gingerbread Fred said . . .

"Ride, ride, ride,
as fast as you can.
You can't catch me,
I'm the gingerbread man!"

Then Gingerbread Fred reached the river,
where a fox sat, watching the fish.
"Need some help?" said the fox.
"Jump on my back.
I can take you across if you wish."

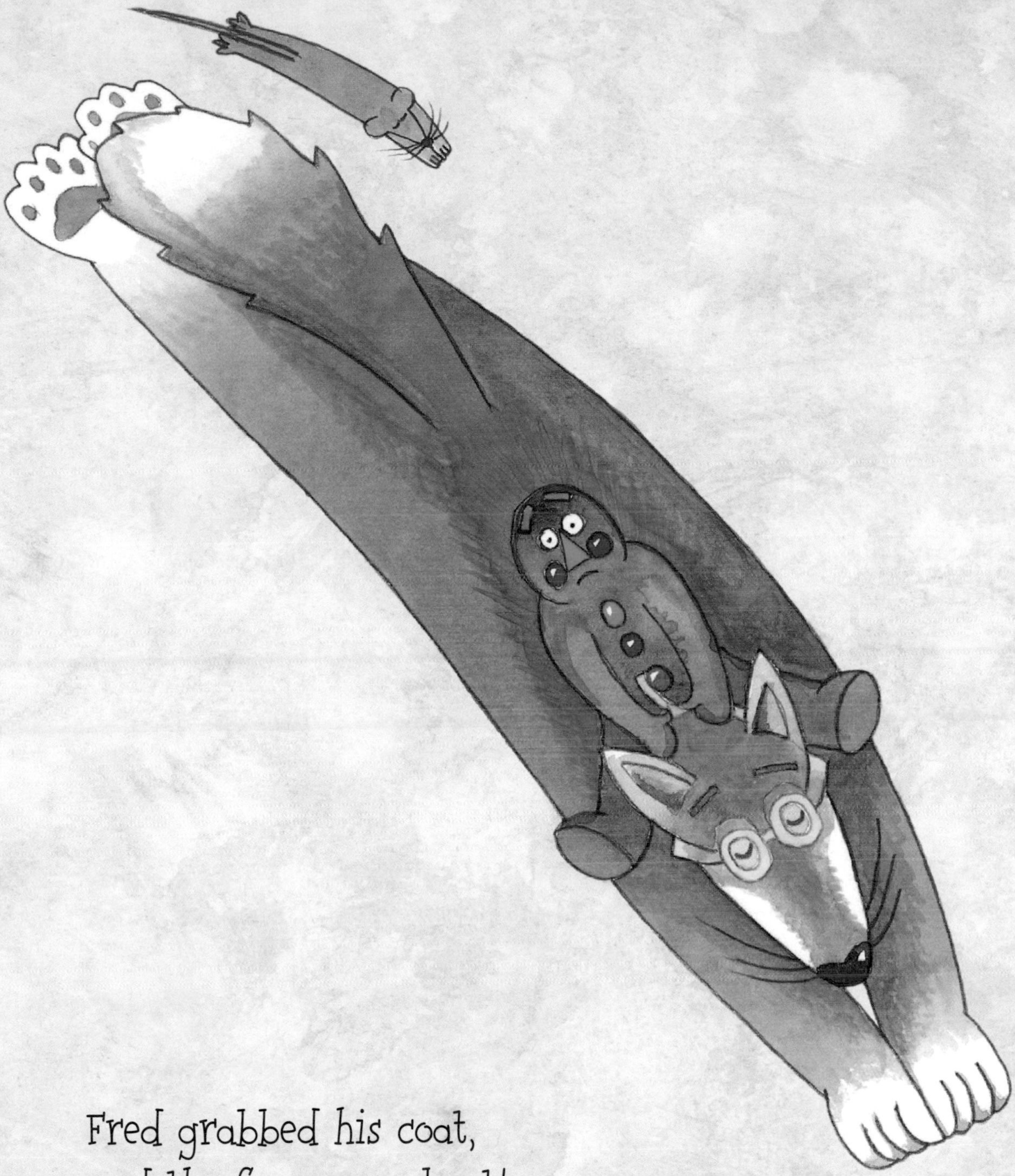

Fred grabbed his coat,
and the fox was a boat!

And Gingerbread Fred said . . .

"Swim, swim, swim,
as fast as you can.
You can't catch me,
I'm the gingerbread man!"

As the water gradually rose,
the fox said to Fred,
“Move up further –
it’s best if you sit on my nose.”

Quite soon they were over the river,
and Gingerbread Fred said, "Good-bye!"
"Not so fast," said the fox.
"There's one more thing.
Now, how would you like to fly?"

And before you could say
"GINGER SNAPS,"
Fred was thrown high up in the sky!

And Gingerbread Fred said . . .

"Fly fly, fly,
as fast as you can.
You can't catch me,
I'm the . . ."

CRUNCH! SCRUNCH! MUNCH!
The fox had him for lunch.

And Gingerbread Fred
said nothing ever again.

This is the story of Crystal Clean,
the sleeping daughter of a king and queen.
Throughout the story, can you guess what?
There's a feather duster for you to spot.

Sleeping Beauty

Nick and Claire Page
Illustrations by Sara Baker

Once a king and queen
held a party on the green,
to celebrate their baby.
They called her Crystal Clean.

They were thrilled to bits!
The king did the splits.
The queen served lots of crackers
with lots of cheesy bits.

Among the many guests
to welcome the princess
were seven kindly fairies,
who came with presents to bless.

Mary
Mary Jo
Mary Beth
Good Dental Care
Beauty
Goodness
Wisdom

A scary fairy came.
Griselda was her name.
She hadn't been invited
but walked in all the same.

"A curse!" Griselda said.
"A curse upon her head!
She'll be pricked by a spindle.
Your baby will be dead!"

"No need for any fears,"
the youngest fairy cheers.
"I'll change this curse, instead
she will sleep for a hundred years."

The queen warns Crystal Clean,
each year till she's sixteen,
"Don't ever touch a spindle.
You don't know where it's been."

But then one night,
to her delight,
the princess found a tower,
and there, shining bright,

a spinning wheel she found,
spinning round and round.
She pricked her little finger
and fell to the ground.

You couldn't hear a peep.
Everybody fell asleep.
The place was filled with snoring
and dreaming deep.

A hundred years went by. The ivy climbed so high,
you'd never know the castle stood nearby.

Then along the forest floor, comes a prince, who finds the door. He cuts through thorns and roses and thinks he hears a snore.

The castle's in a mess.
The prince finds the princess.
He falls in love, he kisses her,
and she wakes up! Success!

KEEP CLOSED
I SAID
DANGER
KEEP OUT
I REPEAT . . .
PLEASE KEEP
DESK TIDY!

He marries Crystal Clean,
and on the village green
they hold the biggest party
that you have ever seen!

This is the story of a room full of straw,
a strange little man, and a magic trapdoor.
You can read it in bed, in a chair, on the floor!
There's something else – can you guess what?
Throughout the story, there's some thread to spot.

Rumpelstiltskin

Nick and Claire Page
Illustrations by Sara Baker

There once was a miller who lied to the king,
"I have a sweet daughter called Geraldine.
She turns yellow straw into gold with one spin!"

The king locked the girl in a room full of straw,
saying, "Spin me gold or you'll die, for sure."
Geraldine wept. Then guess what she saw!

From a door in the floor, a little man sprang,
"Spin straw into gold? Why, do it I can!
Give me your necklace, and I am your man!"

Geraldine promised, and so he sang,
"Yellow straw, threads of gold!
Spinning magic now behold!"
And the straw turned to gold.
Then he left through the door in the floor.

The king was delighted with his golden thread.
"Now spin this lot, too," he greedily said,
"in time for tomorrow, or off with your head!"

The miller's girl cried when she saw more straw.
Then out came the man from his magic trapdoor:
"Give me your ring, and I'll help you once more."

Geraldine promised, and so he sang,
"Yellow straw, threads of gold!
Spinning magic now behold!"

And the straw turned to gold.
Then he left through the door in the floor.

The king gave her more straw.
"Here, have one last try!"
Then went off again, as the girl gave a sigh,
"I have nothing to pay with. I'll have to die!"

When the little man saw the straw in a pile,
he gave her a look, both cunning and wild.
"Do it I will, but I'll have your first child!"

Sadly, Geraldine promised.
And so he sang:
"Yellow straw, threads of gold!
Spinning magic now behold!"
And the straw turned to gold.
Then he left through the door in the floor.

The girl married the king, had a baby next year,
and she'd almost forgotten the feeling of fear,
when from his trapdoor, the man reappeared.

"I've come for that baby, asleep in the bed!"
"Not Gerald!" cried Geraldine. "Take me instead!"
"I'll give you a test," the little man said.

"For three days at sunset, I'll visit again,
and give you three chances
to guess my real name.
Get it wrong, and the baby is mine all the same."
And he left through the door in the floor.

The queen sent servants to find out his name,
but they had no answer when he came again.
"Is it Caspar?" she asked. "Or Bert? Or Elaine?"

"WRONG!" said the little man.
And he left through the door in the floor.

Next day was no better, and when he arrived,
the queen couldn't guess it, hard though she tried!
"Leonardo?" she asked. "Or Jones? Or McBride?"

"WRONG AGAIN!" said the little man.
And he left through the door in the floor.

By now, the queen thought her hopes were all shot,
but then came a messenger, sweaty and hot.
"My Lady!" he cried. "We've hit the jackpot!"

"In a house by the mountains, I saw a wee man,
shouting with glee at his wild, cunning plan.
Singing, 'Guess she will not. Rumpelstiltskin I am!'"

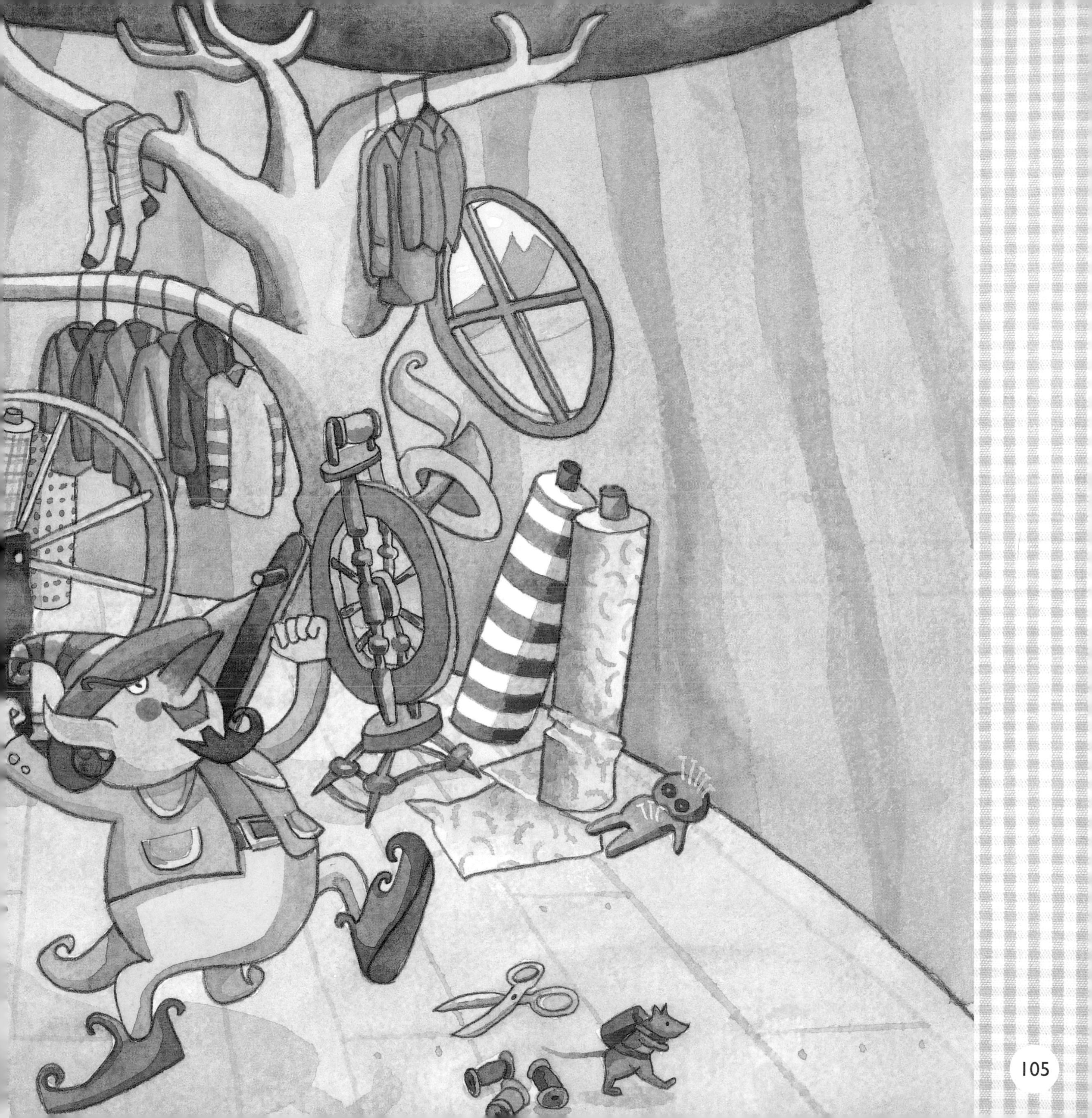

That evening, as Geraldine poured out some wine,
the little gold spinner appeared right on time.
"Last chance!" he said. "Then the boy will be mine!
Or if it's too difficult, then just give in."

"Not so fast," said the queen.
"Let the wheel have a spin.
Is it Boris?
Or Britney?
Or RUMPELSTILTSKIN?"

Rumpelstiltskin cried, "Noooooooo!"
Then he bounced round the room,
he swelled like a toad, and his head turned maroon.
And BANG! Rumpelstiltskin burst like a balloon!

Now the point of this story, we must say to you,
is: Don't ever lie about things you can't do.
Don't be greedy for gold, even if you're a king,
and never trust someone called . . .
RUMPELSTILTSKIN!

This is the story of Princess Snow White.
Read it during the day, or read it at night.
There's something else – can you guess what?
On every page, there's a cat to spot!

Snow White

Nick and Claire Page
Illustrations by Sara Baker

Once there was a young princess with
skin as white as snow, lips as red as
blood, and hair as black as ebony.
She was called Snow White.

Her mother was dead, and her father had married again.
The new queen was beautiful but vain.
Every day she asked, "Mirror, mirror on the wall,
who is the fairest of them all?"
And the mirror replied,
"You, Oh Queen, are the fairest, it's true,
No one else looks as good as you."

As each year passed, Snow White
grew more beautiful. One day,
the queen said to her mirror,
"Mirror, mirror on the wall,
who is the fairest of them all?"

The mirror answered,
"You, Oh Queen, are a lovely sight,
but if you force me to choose,
I'll go for Snow White."
The queen turned yellow
with shock, then green
with envy.

So she ordered a huntsman to take Snow White into the forest and kill her. But the huntsman felt sorry for Snow White and let her go. She ran through the forest until she came to a tiny house.

Inside there was a table with seven places and seven little beds. Snow White lay on the beds and fell asleep.

Later, seven dwarfs came home from digging in the mines. They were surprised to find Snow White in their home!

"Who are you?" she asked.
"We are Monday, Tuesday,
Wednesday, Thursday, Friday,
Saturday, and Fred," they said.

The dwarfs agreed to let Snow White stay
to take care of the house and cook their meals.

Back at the palace, the queen asked again,
"Mirror, mirror on the wall, who is the
fairest of them all?"

And the mirror replied,
"You, Oh Queen, have the beauty of night,
but you're still coming second to Princess
Snow White. She's still alive and still good-looking.
She lives with the dwarfs and does their cooking."

The Queen turned
purple with passion
and red with rage.

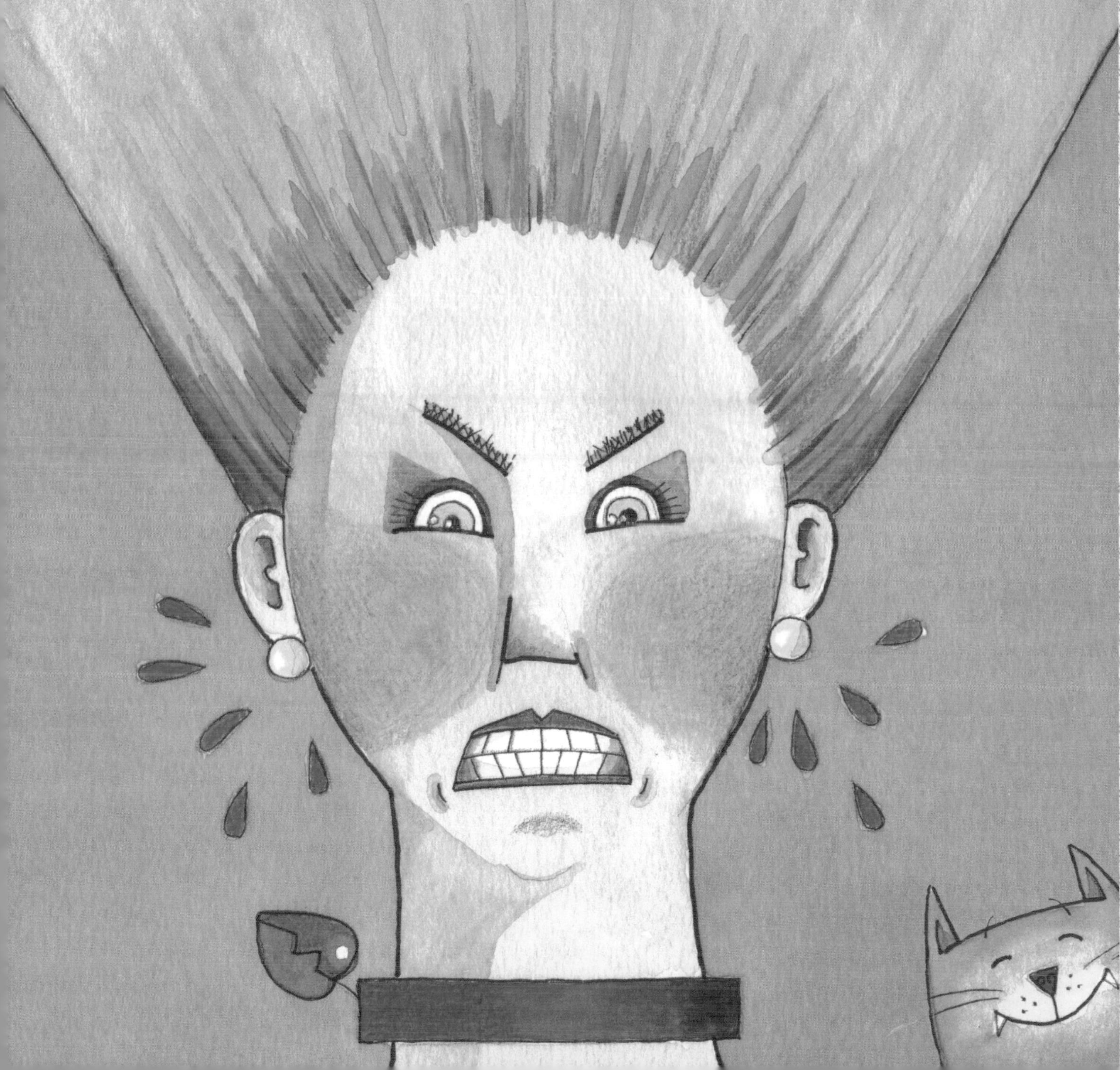

So, using her magic, she went to the
cottage, disguised as an old woman:
"Try my apples. Take a bite!
Just the thing for skin so white!"

Snow White didn't know it was the queen, so she bought a juicy red apple. But the apple was poisoned, and when Snow White took a bite, she fell down as if dead.

The dwarfs found Snow White
lying on the ground.
"She's dead!" cried Monday,
Tuesday, Wednesday, Thursday,
Friday, Saturday, and Fred.

They put her in a glass coffin
and took turns to guard it.

The queen ran back to the palace.
"Mirror, mirror on the wall,
who is the fairest of them all?"

And the mirror replied sadly,
"You, Oh Queen, are the fairest of fair.
Snow White's dead, so what do I care?"

One day, a prince came riding through the forest and saw Snow White lying there, her skin as white as snow, lips as red as blood, and hair as black as ebony. At once, he fell in love. "Let me take her back to my castle," he begged. "I cannot live without her."

As his servants lifted the coffin, one tripped, and the piece of poisoned apple fell out of Snow White's mouth.

At once, Snow White woke up!
"She's not dead!" cried Monday,
Tuesday, Wednesday, Thursday,
Friday, Saturday, and Fred.

Back at the castle, as usual,
the queen asked her mirror,
"Mirror, mirror on the wall,
Who is the fairest of them all?"
And the mirror answered,
"You, Oh Queen, are far from plain,
but Snow White is alive again!"
At this, the queen turned
every color under the sun
all at once, until she shattered
into a thousand pieces.

So Snow White married the prince. And the seven dwarfs came and saw them every day: Monday, Tuesday, Wednesday, Thursday, Friday, Saturday, and Fred.

This is the story of Three Billy Goats Gruff.
You can read it yourself –
it's not very tough.
Why not give it a try,
if you're brave enough!
One thing more – can you guess what?
On every page, there's a worm to spot!

Three Billy Goats Gruff

Nick and Claire Page
Illustrations by Katie Saunders

In the valley, by a river,
lived three happy billy goats.
One was small: Little Will,
with a bell around his throat.
One was tall: Brother Bill,
with a big and shaggy coat.
One was HUGE: Rough Tough Gruff.
He could turn you into fluff!

On the mountain, by a bridge,
lived a nasty troll called Sid.
He had eyes – big as pies,
ears like two big saucepan lids,
yellow teeth, wrinkly throat,
and his favorite food was goat!

In the valley, one fine day,
there was not much grass around.
"Time to go," said Little Will.
"Let's climb up to higher ground.
Cross the bridge, to the pass
where there's loads of lovely grass!"

So the three goats trotted off,
to the bridge, up by the pass.
"I'll go first," said Little Will.
Look at all that lovely grass."
Trip-trap-trip! As he ran,
Sid the Troll jumped out and sang . . .

"Don't want chicken,
don't want lamb,
don't want bacon,
don't want ham.
Don't want turkey,
or beef, or pork.
Want some goat
upon my fork!"

No trespassing

Little Will sweetly smiled, and he gave a little bleat.
"Don't have me for your tea; I am not much good to eat.
But if goat is your prize, why not try some Goat Surprise?"

"Goat Surprise?" said the troll.
"Oooh, that sounds completely yummy!"
"Just you wait," said Little Will,
"and you'll have some in your tummy.
My big bro' can tell you more
about this meal so scrummy.
Let me through, if you will."
And he crossed onto the hill.

Brother Bill came along
with his great big shaggy coat.
And up and onto the bridge,
went this brave, strong billy goat.
Trip-trap-trip! As he ran,
Sid the Troll jumped out and sang . . .

"Don't want apples,
don't want cherries,
don't want peaches,
don't want berries.
Don't want plums, or grapes, or prunes.
Want some goat upon my spoon!"

Brother Bill calmly stood
and he gave a little baa.
"Don't have me for your tea;
eating me won't get you far.
But to fill your insides,
you should try some Goat Surprise."

"Goat Surprise?" said the troll.
"Ooooh! Sounds absolutely great!"
"In a mo'," said Brother Bill,
"you will have some on your plate!
My big brother will be here.
All you have to do is wait.
Let me through, let me pass."
And he went to eat some grass.

Rough Tough Gruff soon appeared,
and up to the bridge he sped.
He was huge, he was fierce,
with great horns upon his head.
Trip-trap-trip! As he ran,
Sid the Troll jumped
out and sang . . .

Keep
off.

"Don't want lettuce, don't want beans,
don't want cabbage, don't want greens.
Don't want carrots, peas, or shallots!
Want some goat here in my pot!"

Rough Tough Gruff just stood still,
and he said to Sid the Troll,
"If it's goat that you want,
you can put me in your bowl.
Pick on someone your own size!
Here's my special Goat Surprise!"

"Goat Surprise?" cried the troll. "Ooooh, it's come my way at last!"
Then he saw Rough Tough Gruff, charging straight for him, fast!
Sid felt sick, when a kick hit him like a mighty blast.
Rough Tough Gruff put Sid in a cast.
Then he went to munch some grass.

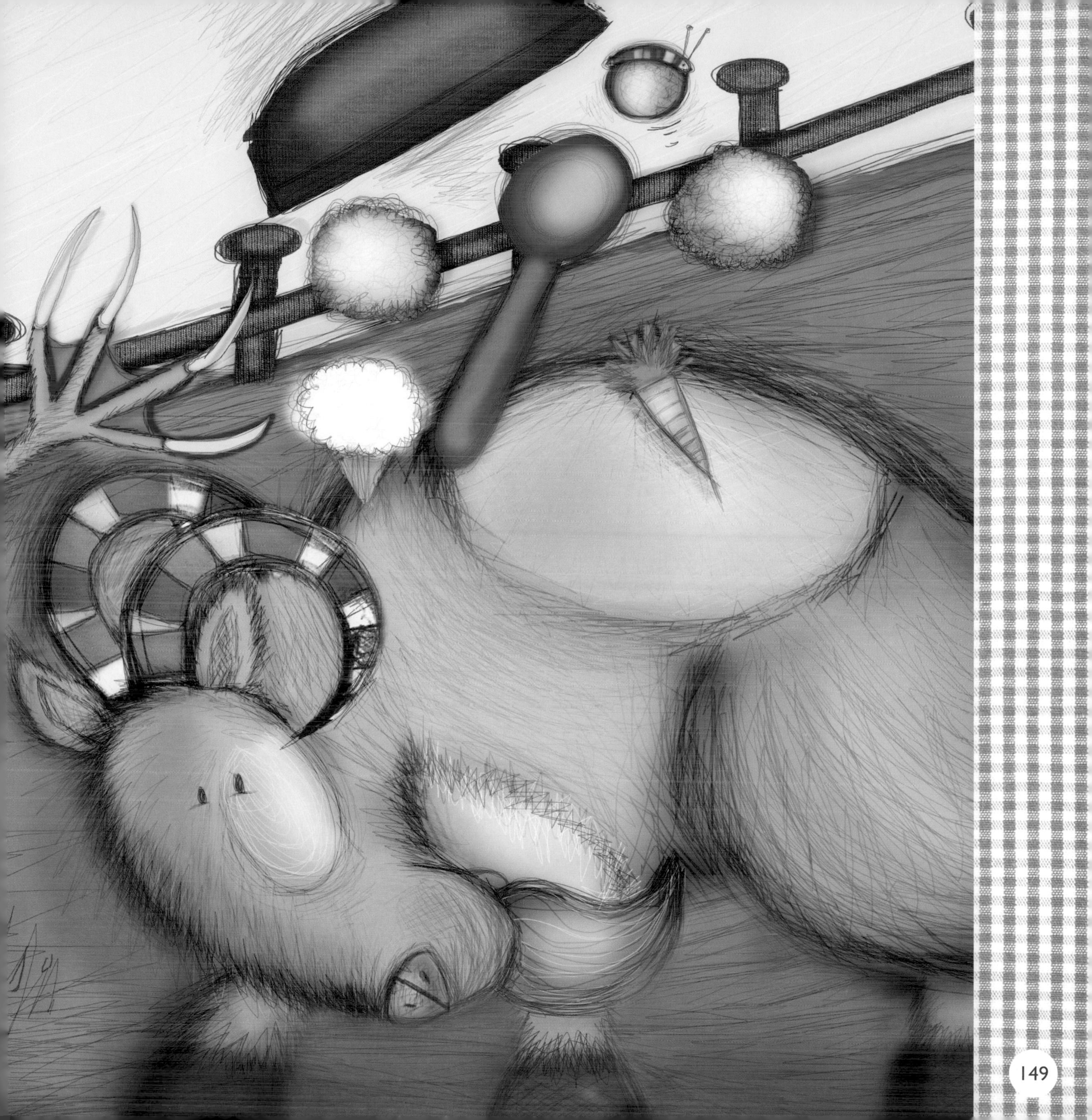

Those three goats set up home,
on that green and grassy hill.
With a munch they had their lunch,
Rough Tough Gruff and Bill and Will.
Sid the Troll disappeared;
all his friends said he was ill.
From then on, you will note,
he couldn't stand the taste of goat.

keep off

This is the story of three little pigs,
and houses built of straw, bricks, and twigs.
There's something else – can you guess what?
Throughout the story, there's a pot to spot!

Three Little Pigs

Nick and Claire Page
Illustrations by Katie Saunders

Three little pigs left home one day,
packed their bags and went on their way.
Mother Pig said, "Good-bye, bye, bye!"
But a wolf saw them go and thought,
"Mmm – PORK PIE!"

Blue Prints
Houses from Straw

Straws 'R' us

Sale
50% off

The first little pig met a man selling straw.
"Will it make a good house? I'm not quite sure."
So he paid for the bales and stacked them high,
but the wolf licked his lips, thinking,
"Mmm – STIR-FRY!"

The second little pig met a man selling wood.
"I think I'll build with this; it looks pretty good."
So he worked all day and did not stop,
but the wolf licked his lips, thinking,
"Mmm – PORK CHOP!"

25% off
Edward Woodwood Supplies
Edward Woodwood Supplies

The third little pig met a man selling bricks.
"These look strong, much better than sticks."
So he built his house, all shiny and new,
but the wolf licked his lips, thinking,
"Mmm – BARBECUE!"

top
sand

Work in
Progress
Keep Out

Mr Wolf's
top ten
pork dishes

When the homes were finished by the piggies three,
they went inside to have some tea.
But the wolf was feeling very hungry, too,
and the wolf licked his lips, thinking,
"Mmm – PORK STEW!"

Said the wolf to Piggy Straw, "Now let me in!"
"Not by the hair on my chinny chin chin!"
So the wolf huffed and puffed,
and the house went WHAM!
And the wolf licked his lips, shouting,
"Mmm – BOILED HAM!"

Piggy Straw ran straight
to the house of Piggy Wood.
And behind him came the wolf,
"Let me in! I'll be good!"

Then he huffed and he puffed,
and the house went SMASH!
And the wolf licked his lips, shouting,
"Mmm – GOULASH!"

Then the two pigs ran
to the house made of bricks.
They were chased by the wolf
(who was not quite as quick).
There he huffed and he puffed,
but the house stayed whole.
So, the wolf climbed the roof, shouting,
"Mmm — CASSEROLE!"

No
Wolves

Then the three pigs ran
and they fetched a pot.
"Quick, quick," said Piggy Bricks,
"let's make it hot!"
As the hungry wolf jumped
down the chimney tower,
he landed in the pot and screamed,
"Oww — SWEET AND SOUR!"

He jumped out quick and ran far away
from the bricks, the wood, and the pile of hay.

And the lesson of this story is –
learn it quick –
don't be a silly sausage –
make your house out of bricks!

This is the story of Goldilocks,
a little girl who never knocks.
And throughout the story,
there's a clock to spot!

Goldilocks and the Three Bears

Nick and Claire Page
Illustrations by Sara Baker

In a house in the woods lived Daddy Bear,
married to Mom with curly hair.
Smallest of all, in the rocking chair,
is their baby, Little Bear Bottom.

It's breakfast time, believe it or not!
The porridge is done, but it's way too hot!
So they go for a walk, while it cools in the pot –
Mom, Dad, and Little Bear Bottom.

Along comes a girl called Goldilocks,
wearing her favorite red and blue socks.
She walks straight in – the girl never knocks!
Her manners are gone – she forgot 'em!

She looks for some porridge, and, guess what!
One's too cold, and one's too hot.
The last is just right, she gobbles the lot.
What a bad little girl – she's rotten!

Feeling full up, she wants to sit down.
"Too hard! Too soft!" she says with a frown.
Tries baby bear's chair and ends upside down!
Crash! She's gone through the bottom!

Sleepy, she goes upstairs to bed.
Too high, too low, two beds hurt her head.
So she picks the little bear's bed instead.
(She likes the sheets – they are cotton.)

The bears come home. The bears are mad!
"Someone's been eating my porridge," says Dad.
"Mine, too," says Mom,
"And mine," says their lad.
"She's eaten it right to the bottom!"

"Someone's been sitting in my chair, too,"
says Dad, then Mom. "Oh, what shall we do?"
"And mine is broken. Boo-hoo! It was new!"
cries sad little Baby Bear Bottom.

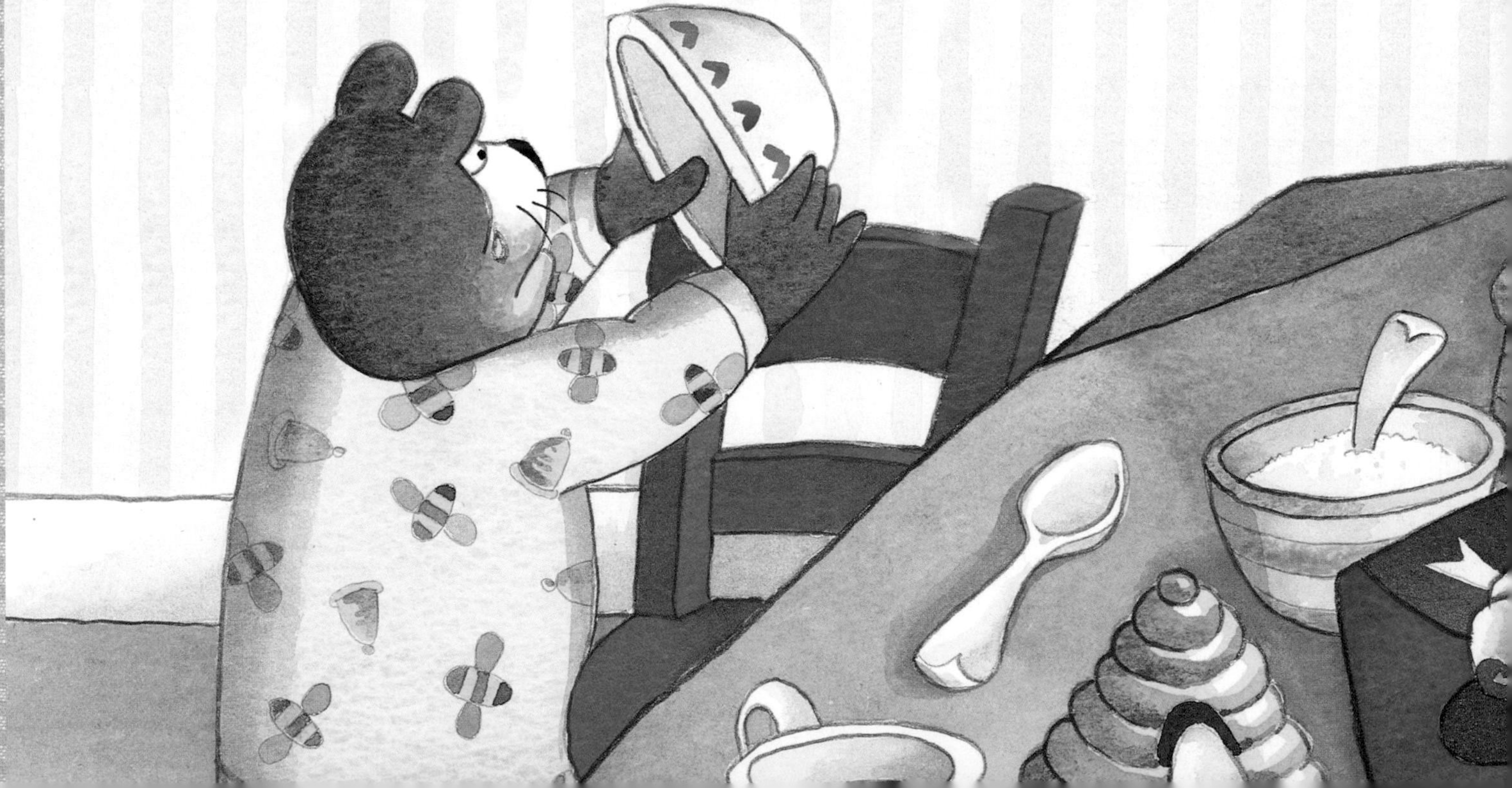

They race up the stairs, and hearing a knock,
Goldilocks suddenly wakes with a shock!
Little Bear screams, and she's up like a shot,
"There's the intruder – we've got 'em!"

Out of the window she jumps – and away!
She learns a lot about bears that day –
their beds, their chairs, and to stay far away
from the porridge of Baby Bear Bottom!